Oh, A-Hunting We Will Go

John Langstaff

Oh,
A-Hunting
We Will Go

pictures by

Nancy Winslow Parker

Aladdin Paperbacks

First Aladdin Paperbacks edition 1991

Text copyright © 1974 by John Langstaff
Illustrations copyright © 1974 by Nancy Winslow Parker

Aladdin Paperbacks
An imprint of Simon & Schuster Children's Publishing Division
1230 Avenue of the Americas
New York, NY 10020

Manufactured in China

14 16 18 20 19 17 15

Library of Congress Cataloging-in-Publication Data
Langstaff, John M.
Oh, a-hunting we will go / John Langstaff; pictures by Nancy
Winslow Parker.
p. cm.
Summary: Old and new verses for a popular folk song about hunting
and capturing an animal–and then letting him go.
ISBN 0-689-71503-X
1. Folk-songs, English–Texts. [1. Folk songs.] I. Parker,
Nancy Winslow, ill. II. Title.
PZ8.3.L280H   1991
782.42162'21041–dc20   91-1987   CIP   AC

*For all the children
who helped me make up extra
verses for this folk song.*

Oh, a-hunting we will go,
 A-hunting we will go;
We'll catch a fox

And put him in a box,
   And then we'll let him go!

Oh, a-hunting we will go,
  A-hunting we will go;
We'll catch a lamb

And put him in a pram,
And then we'll let him go!

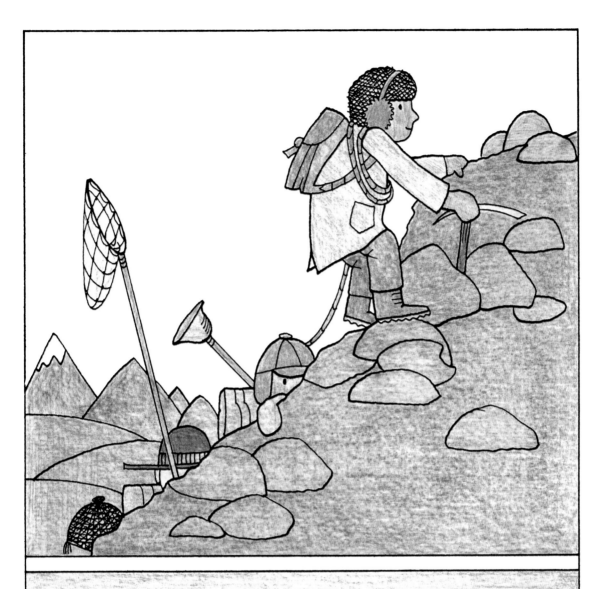

Oh, a-hunting we will go,
A-hunting we will go;
We'll catch a goat

And put him in a boat,
And then we'll let him go!

Oh, a-hunting we will go,
  A-hunting we will go;
We'll catch a bear

And put him in underwear,
And then we'll let him go!

Oh, a-hunting we will go,
A-hunting we will go;
We'll catch a whale

And put him in a pail,
And then we'll let him go!

Oh, a-hunting we will go,
   A-hunting we will go;
We'll catch a snake

And put him in a cake,
And then we'll let him go!

Oh, a-hunting we will go,
   A-hunting we will go;
We'll catch a mouse

And put him in a house,
  And then we'll let him go!

Oh, a-hunting we will go,
   A-hunting we will go;
We'll catch a pig

And put him in a wig,

And then we'll let him go!

Oh, a-hunting we will go,
  A-hunting we will go;
We'll catch a skunk

And put him in a bunk,
  And then we'll let him go!

Oh, a-hunting we will go,
    A-hunting we will go;
We'll catch an armadillo

And put him in a pillow,
And then we'll let him go!

Oh, a-hunting we will go,
  A-hunting we will go;
We'll catch a fish

And put him in a dish,
  And then we'll let him go!

Oh, a-hunting we will go,
  A-hunting we will go;
We'll catch a brontosaurus

And put him in a chorus,
    And then we'll let him go!

Oh, a-hunting we will go,
  A-hunting we will go;
We'll just pretend and in the end,
  We'll always let them go!

Oh, A-Hunting We Will Go

Oh, a - hunt - ing we will go, A -
hunt - ing we will go; We'll catch a fox and
put him in a box, And then we'll let him go!

We'll catch a lamb and put him in a pram,
And then we'll let him go!

We'll catch a goat and put him in a boat,
And then we'll let him go!

We'll catch a bear and put him in underwear
And then we'll let him go!

We'll catch a whale and put him in a pail,
And then we'll let him go!

We'll catch a snake and put him in a cake,
And then we'll let him go!

We'll catch a mouse and put him in a house,
And then we'll let him go!

We'll catch a pig and put him in a wig,
And then we'll let him go!

We'll catch a skunk and put him in a bunk,
And then we'll let him go!

We'll catch an armadillo and put him in a pillow,
And then we'll let him go!

We'll catch a fish and put him in a dish,
And then we'll let him go!

We'll catch a brontosaurus and put him in a choru...
And then we'll let him go!

We'll just pretend and in the end,
We'll always let them go!